This book belongs to

....

Mia

Mia

Ellie

Written with love for a girl called Alice
With thanks to some wonderful members of
the Society of Children's Book Writers and Illustrators,
my friend Carol
and husband Neil
End papers by Mia Holloway, aged 7
and Ellie Gough, aged 6

Published by Skelwicks Arts
www.neeliewicks.com
Copyright © 2017 Neelie Wicks

ISBN 978-0-9957721-0-6

Miss Pickle
a Dizzy Witch

Written by Neelie Wicks

Illustrated by
Dawn Treacher

Miss Pickle lived at the end of Parsley Lane with her best friends, Nutmeg and Pepper.

She couldn't do her spells without them.

Now it was time to make a spell for breakfast.

But Nutmeg was hiding.
Miss Pickle was hungry and cross.
"Where is that crazy, lazy cat?" she asked.

Pepper stood on his head
and tried to think ...
but could only think of cheese.

"We'll just have to make a spell to find a cat," said Miss Pickle.

"Eeh, oh noO, spells come out wrong when Nutmeg's not here to help," thought Pepper.

Then suddenly...

... Miss Pickle grabbed Pepper by the tail and dangled him over the magic washer.

"Dingle, dangle, what a tangle," squeaked Pepper, as he shook in a spell to find a cat.

"**E**ggy, peggy, smelly welly, spin that spell and let's get ready!" Miss Pickle shouted.

"Now let's make a brew that's as good as stew, in goes a peg, then an egg, now a kipper and a flipper!"

But, oh nO!

Magic bits and pieces leapt in and out of the magic washer as it spun the stew.

"Spelks! That's not right. Bother!" Miss Pickle cried.

"QUICK, Pepper! PUT IT RIGHT!" "Dingle, dangle, unspin that tangle," squealed Pepper.

But, oh nO! OUT SHOT ... the peg, egg, flipper and kipper ...

... and something else ... ... out sprung a spring.

Pepper stood on his head for safety.

Then he started hopping like a bunny.

"Spelks! That's not right either," shrieked Miss Pickle.

But then ...

... Pepper hopped and flopped right out the door, up Parsley Lane, around the bend and through the park, to find his friend.

"Yippee!"

"A hopping spell is just the trick to find that crazy, lazy cat."

Parsley Lane

There he was, peeking out of the biggest, big tree.

"Help me! I hid and now I'm stuck. Ouch! This blackbird keeps pecking me."

"You're a very naughty cat to hide," squealed Pepper.

"You'll just have to jump. One, two, three!"

"Without a parachute?
But I'm ssscccared."

"This is an **emergency**,"
thought Pepper and he hopped off home for help.

Miss Pickle was very worried to hear about Nutmeg and she was very worried about making a spell to help.

T his washer's going wonky, Pepper,"
said Miss Pickle, as she swept the floor.

"I think we've had a **disaster.**"

Pepper thought so too, as he
went to fetch another spell.

"Oh, Pepper!" cried Miss Pickle.
"A rescue spell. You clever mouse!"

"Dingle, dangle, mingle, mangle,"
squeaked Pepper,
as he shook in
a spell to
rescue a cat.

"Eggy, peggy, smelly welly,
spin that spell and let's get ready!" Miss Pickle shouted.

Then Miss Pickle threw in some soap and then a rope and
three red jam sandwiches.

Pepper stood on his head for safety
as the magic washer spun the stew.

Whoosh, gurgle,
whizzzz, wheeee, thump.

POP!

"Oh no!" Pepper cried. "It's a **flying** spell, not a rescue spell."

"Even better," chuckled Miss Pickle, as the laundry baskets jiggled up and down.

Round and round the room they flew before landing with a bump.

"Quick, get in for take-off!
Grab the washing line."

Vroom,
whoosh,
zooomm!

And off they shot to the
biggest, big tree.

"Yahoo!" cackled Miss Pickle, as she lassoed the tree top.

Then Nutmeg set off on a perilous journey as he clung and hung, then crawled along the line...

... Until he fell!

Right into the pink, frilly knickers!

"**Attention, attention!** Make way for the knickers!
they yelled at the blackbird who looked on in fright."

So, with legs in the pants and pegs to keep steady, Nutmeg was hauled onto the flight.

"Thank you, oh thank you! I really am sorry," said Nutmeg.

"Grumble, grrrumble," gurgled three empty tummies.

"Will I be forgiven if we make ONE BIG SPELL for breakfast, lunch AND tea?" asked Nutmeg.

"YES!" the other two agreed.

"And we'll eat it for SUPPER!" chuckled Miss Pickle, as they flew home to Parsley Lane.

The magical fun doesn't end here; you can collect more
Miss Pickle stories.

The Miss Pickle series:

Miss Pickle a Dizzy Witch

Miss Pickle's Invitation from Queen Ethel

Miss Pickle's Space Mission

And that's not all! If you like cooking as well as reading, ask a
grown-up to help you make Nutmeg's Magic Flipper Kippers!

Nutmeg's Magic Flipper Kippers

Magic Bits and Pieces:

1 grown-up
Oven gloves
Toaster
Microwave
Grill
Wooden spoon, fork, plate
Big bowl, medium bowl and small bowl
Pastry brush
Paper towel and foil

Magic Ingredients:

1 tin of tuna
1 slice of bread
1 potato
1 egg
2 tablespoons of red sauce
2 tablespoons of oil
Pepper
4 magic eyes
(grown-ups think these are currants)

How to make the Magic Flipper Kippers:

First, get your Magic Bits and Pieces together, including the grown-up. Next, get your Magic Ingredients ready. If you have an apron like Miss Pickle, put it on.

Prick the potato with the fork 3 times and wrap it in the paper towel. With help, set the microwave on high and cook it for 5 minutes, or until squashy. Using the gloves, put the potato into the medium size bowl, take the paper off and cover with the plate, then leave to cool a little.

Toast the bread in the toaster. Cover the grill pan with the foil.

Ask the grown-up to open the tin of tuna and drain off the liquid. Tip it into the big bowl and add the red sauce. Crack the egg into the small bowl, then tip it into the big bowl and shake in some pepper. Mix with the fork to make a goo.

Break the toast into tiny crumbs with your hands, then add to the goo and mix with the spoon. Next, using the fork, smash the potato up to make lumpy, mashed potato. Add this to the goo and do a big mix up.

Divide the goo into 4 blobs. Make each blob into the shape of a kipper and stick in an eye. Brush oil all over the kippers and put them on the foil. With help, turn the grill on medium hot and cook the kippers for 10 minutes on each side, or until they are golden brown. EAT THEM!

Shout EGGY, PEGGY, SMELLY WELLY if you enjoyed them!

Or, SPELKS if you didn't!

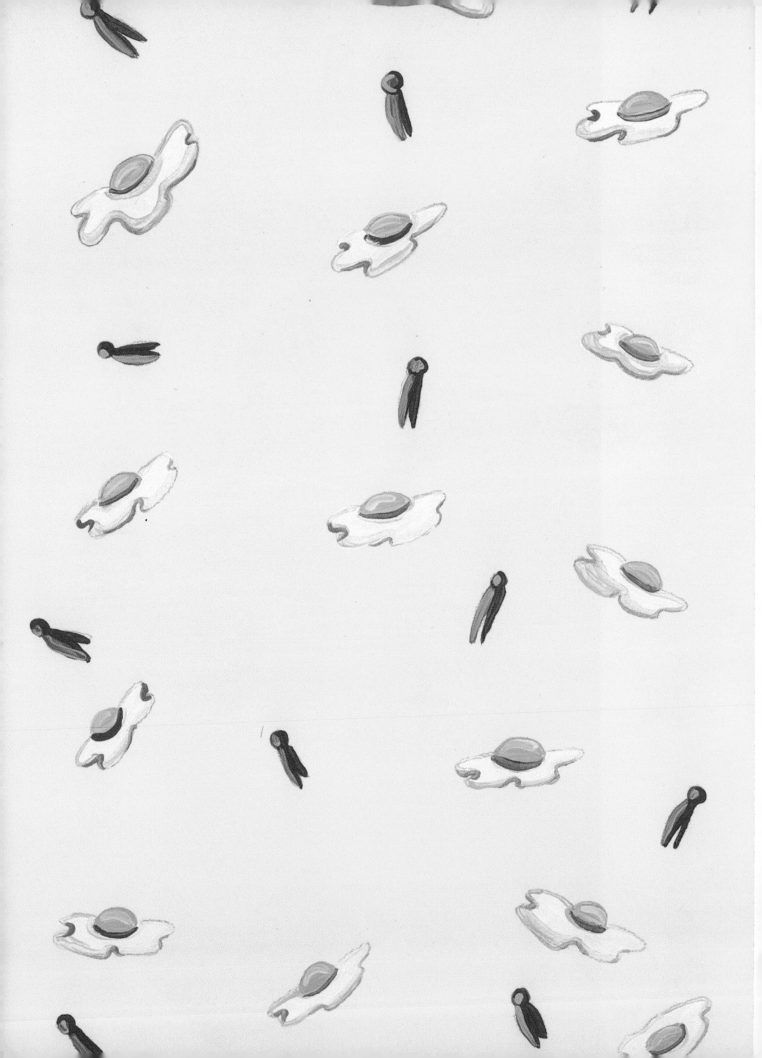